welcome to
CHRISTIANIA

fred leebron

Outpost19 | San Francisco
outpost19.com

Leebron, Fred
    Welcome to Christiania / Fred Leebron
    ISBN 9781937402853 (pbk)
    ISBN 9781937402850 (ebk)

Library of Congress Control Number: 2015912532

SHORT-ISH
SERIES

OUTPOST19

ORIGINAL
PROVOCATIVE
READING

SHORT-ISH
NOVELLAS
EXTENDED ESSAYS

welcome to
CHRISTIANIA

For Kathryn, Cade, Jacob and Benjamin

PART I

one

These people who think they are something, they are really not. They come and go wrapped like gypsies at a carnival, sounding like artists, smelling of mildew. I can't take them anymore.

Yesterday I sat in the bakery, eating bread. Everyone kept coming in: Jens and Vincent and Carla and Flavia and people whose names I didn't even know. Their pants had pockets on the thighs and shins and buttocks. Their skirts swished over flowered longjohns. I couldn't take it, so I left.

On Pusher Street all the tables were taken. It felt awful to stand there without a table to protect me. And it was too warm to peddle in the Common Kitchen, so I didn't try to sell anything. I went home and fell asleep.

I am sick today. Sick with paranoia. When I get like this, I usually take a whore and feel better. But not today. Today I will lie in bed and think until I can think no more. Let me tell you what I think.

I think I am nothing. I think if I let them, my own hands would strangle me. Sometimes when I pick my nose my fingers stiffen and plunge further up, bleeding me until I stop them, stop myself.

I am here not because I want to be, but because I have to be. Don't get me wrong. This place is no prison.

It is a...

Sometimes I am coherent. I can think like a rock, I think so clearly. But mostly, oh, it's the paranoia. Every time I feel on the verge of a deep revelation, I fall into it. It swallows me like a mud pit. I am choked and can say nothing.

Unlike all the other pushers, I have no dog. I am my own dog.

Maybe I should say how I got into this...If I can get it out, then maybe I can get out.

I was looking around. The world is not the place it used to be. I have read books that say the world is the most incredible place ever. Well, it's not. Nothing there is incredible. Everything there has happened, and nothing is left.

So I was looking around, looking for it. The usual places: the Andes, Ledakh, Katmandhu, Tibet, the Bush. I couldn't find anything. Nothing.

I was in Copenhagen, on my way to the Faero Islands, and a ruby-haired wench selling jewelry on the Stroeget told me about this place. I came.

In the beginning, it was incredible. You walked the streets of Copenhagen, dulled by gray buildings, bakeries wrapped in glass and steel, supermarkets beneath flat white-trimmed sale signs, clothing stores thronged with wool-coated hangers; and suddenly you stepped through a gate, and you were here. Christiania. It was like going back in time and going forward, too, at once.

I cannot describe it, except...

No, description requires too much revelation, and I am falling into it, falling back into myself struggling in the mud pit. I will try later, all at once, without waiting, without leading up to it.

two

I cannot stand it here any longer. The people are in a socializing frenzy, asking each other to dinner or tea. I did not come here for company. I came here for solitude. We should live in separate caves and meet only at restricted times—not for dinner and never over tea.

We all live here to be different. Some of us are more different than others. Otto says it cannot go on like this. He occupies the hammock in front of the Grocer's. In the winter he has only his long beard and tweed overcoat to keep him warm. He will not come live with me. I have not asked him, because I know he will refuse. He is so big and full of paranoia. I love him.

When I worked at the bakery he loved me, too. I gave him fresh bread for free. The work was hard, though, from two in the morning until ten at night. No one wanted to have fun. They only wanted to make money. Money, money, money. We were supposed to be a collective. Christiania was supposed to be a commune. None of it happened.

Oh yes. We all made the same money at the bakery. We overcharged and cut costs whenever possible. It made me a little sick, but the people made me sicker. Everyone wanted to make the bread "really nice," make it look good, so it would sell well. The pastries would be sprayed with swirls of chocolate and vanilla, topped with strawberry caps and pineapple rings. The french bread would rise an arm's length and look as golden as sunstruck sand. It would all taste like cardboard. They only thought of selling. Baker whores.

I quit and went to see the Big Man. The Big Man has office hours at Woodstock every afternoon from two to four. He is a shriveled worm of a man, obscured by german shepherds and doberman pinschers.

I waited my turn. It was in the summer and the stench of piss was foul. Loud music rang in my ears, and by the time I got introduced, I could not hear myself think.

"Let me see your hands," the Big Man said.

I laid them on the table like pieces of ivory. The dogs ignored me.

"You can always tell a man by his hands," the Big Man said. "Where are you from?"

I told him.

"If you are caught the worst thing will be some days in jail and then deportation. Scare you?"

I shook my head, but it did. I had been here for a year, and hadn't left Christiania once. I didn't know whether I could live outside it. But I shook my head.

He told me something about how much I should sell, and that he would keep his eye on me. He did not scare me. There are only a thousand of us living here, no escape from anybody's eyes. The favorite pastime is gossip. At the bakery, after money, it was all I ever heard of conversation.

So I've been pushing for another two years...But here,

what is time? Old Otto doesn't even know how long he's been here.

Today is like any other day. The tourists are everywhere. Old people out for a stroll, high school expeditions, undercover policemen. They treat us like an open-air museum.

But we are more like a town after a bomb has dropped. Most of our buildings lie in ruins. All of us suffer weird traumas. We have no lights for the nighttime.

In the winter bonfires burn on our streets.

Our violent fields heave in fruitless humps.

The main throughway is a broken road of bottlecaps and cobblestone.

Piles of trash are heaped everywhere.

Incidentally, my mother died when I was two. My father drank himself silly in bars. I left home at sixteen. It is easy to make it around the world without money. Many people are willing to exploit you. I lived with a painter for several years, whose main objective was to wrestle with the snake in my pants.

I searched for places as bleak and as full of possibilities as the night. Katmandhu was full of chickens. I got lice in Ledahk.

    All the women wearing mittens
     All the men without socks...

Only Christiania held me, swallowed me like my own

revelation. Drugs helped. I did lots of them, all kinds. Never was an addict. Could stop any time for however long I felt like it.

The Big Man likes me.

"I trust you," he said the other day.

"I sell well," I said.

"That, too."

I am charmed by his mangy appearance. He wears a 1940's black, pin-striped suit and purple socks. His shoes are beat-up loafers missing the tassels. Shirtless and with silver wings of hair growing on the sides of his head, the Big Man does not aspire to anything but money. But he does not live here, either. He lives in a whale of a house in the city. I have eaten dinner there twice—Pusher of the Month honors.

The Big Man likes Otto, too. They enjoy sharing lunch and a chillum. Sometimes I watch. The Big Man grunts. Otto talks in sentence fragments, mostly nouns.

"Disgust Sin Devil The Fun Is," Otto says.

The Big Man nods. Maybe they are talking code. Otto is so big he can talk anything.

I love you, Otto.

Love is like a sailboat full of wind, cutting across the sea, soaring to the stars. But as soon as it lifts off the water, it bellyflops down. That is what love is like.

We are sitting on a picnic table outside of Moonfisher. Otto is explaining life.

"Christ Sins Thorns In My Side," he says. "Jews Man Lifeboats." His voice rings like a gravel pit.

Won't you hold me, Otto. Please?

The Irish priest is here again. I see him running past the Grocer's, being chased by his flock. Even the Irish live here. They own farms and grow potatoes that look like bull's testicles.

"Repent!" the priest shouts out of breath as he runs, not daring to turn. The sun makes his black frock sheer, and I can see the nipples of his breasts.

"Fuck you!" the Irish scream. The men wear beards and the women have licorice hair. Every month the priest returns to claim his flock, and every month they drive him back into Copenhagen. But he never gives up. Some day, I think, he will inspire a crucifixion.

There is too much religion in the world. Personally, I aspire to internal spirituality. Nothing, nobody, outside of me matters. Except Otto. Otto is as religious as I get. His aviator cap is like a halo and his tweed overcoat is the vestment of a new savior. But there is too much talk about religion and not enough talk about faith. I, too, am full of anecdotes but without one developed plot.

three

Everyone wants to know what it is like to live in anarchy. Let me tell you, it's no big deal. We all have daily routines, postures, objectives that supercede idealized anarchy. And the power-grabbers make sure that there is more "we rule" than self-rule.

I am generalizing. Sorry. I realize this place has its virtues. Otto could not exist anywhere else. You cannot go howling sentence fragments all day out in the real world without somebody arresting you. But in here you can.

And me, could I exist elsewhere? Probably not. Like I said, the real world is not the place it used to be. But in here, in Christiania, it is strange enough. Too much happens—that's true. And often people here subsist on an incredible self-love. They feed on their egoism like desperate wolves caught in a trap feed on themselves. But Christiania is where I live. It is a comet in the sky, falling fast. It is like eating too much candy. It is drugs and farms and pastel colors til you puke.

It is the child of civilization.

Today, the Uro came. There were sixteen of them, marching in rows of four. They kept in step. I was watching from the secret alcove with a couple other pushers. We were laughing and ordering all the dogs to attack, but they ignored us.

We stopped talking when we saw Otto. He was making for the Uro like a drunk polar bear.

"Good Christ Jesus Praised Be Uro Lord Vice," Otto roared.

I tried to shut my eyes but couldn't.

"Clay Dung Human Crap Uro Smells Of—" But their clubs knee-jerked from their sides, and Otto subsided to a growl. When they were finished the mouth of his silver beard had turned purple.

The Uro slinked off like bad children. I rushed out to Otto, crumbs of hash trailing in the cobblestone.

He was laughing, his teeth smeared vermillion and his lips like raw meat. I tried to clean him up. He bellowed something unintelligible.

I was crying. My tears made his nose run. The other pushers giggled. It began to snow. I was making a mess of everything and people were laughing at me.

I am hiding now in one of the abandoned munitions dumps, my knees drawn up to my chest, warming myself in the dark.

No one will come look for me. No one cares about me.

I want to be alone.

I need to be loved. What does it feel like?

You can cry so loudly that no one will hear you. Or you can whisper so softly that the whole world will come to comfort you.

Otto lies in the Health House, breathing like a gravel pit. Many people attend him. The Big Man nervously twirls his gold watch. I know it. I see so well in the dark.

I would masturbate if I could. To be so fully alone like this, the goose pimples rising up and down my arms. It makes me hard.

I am almost happy.

I sat with Otto in the Common Kitchen today. He scared all my clients away, but I did not mind. We had our own table with a lit candle stuck in a wine bottle. Sometimes I held Otto's hand without him noticing.

It is a hand like a shell on a beach, cracked but smooth. I took it to my ear and the roar of the ocean washed over me. Otto was cursing.

I dropped the hand and it swatted me on the breast, chucked my chin, then swiped my beer. Otto is a devil.

I hang out in the bakery to keep warm.

The Baker Whores are busy. Christmas is coming. Jens speculates that they can make a lot of money. When he is not looking, I steal a ten crown coin from the box. Then, as he goes to deliver bread at the Grocer's, I give him the coin and ask him to buy me a pack of cigarettes. He says, okay.

The bell rings at the shop window. No one else here; I have to answer it. One of the bikers wants something. His arms are lined with graying tatoos, and his thick waist is ringed by a leather strap studded with metal balls.

"A berliner," he says.

I give it to him.

"How much?"

"Five crowns," I whisper.

He gives me five crowns. He is a member of the big gang. They never used to pay, but now they occupy a house in Christiania, and are trying to be responsible. They look like they're in pain.

Jens comes back with my cigarettes, and I excuse myself.

The Full Moon party yesterday at Arne's was awful. Everyone wore a costume but me. I went for the booze. Otto stumbled in later, wearing his aviator cap. He looked himself and everyone comforted him. He roared his regrets that he could not come, even though he was already there. They all laughed and started plying him with Full Moon Punch—a biodynamic cocktail containing homemade alcohol.

Half the people were dressed like David Bowie, smoking clove cigarettes. No one talked to me. I hung on the fringe of the circle surrounding Otto, and drank the punch from a styrofoam cup.

Some of the Baker Whores did start to approach me, but I sneered at them. They're looking for more people to work the Christmas Market. Not me.

After midnight, in the spirit of things, another pusher offered me a bargain on mushrooms and I accepted.

I ate them right there. Soon my gut began to roar and heat rushed to my face. I thanked the pusher and slipped out for a walk.

I stumbled out to the ruins and listened to the Greenlanders standing around an open fire, passing whiskey. They are pathetic people with faces like walruses, and I like them a lot. But they smell of piss. I can stand them only in the outdoors.

They had a chillum and I ingratiated myself by filling a round. They continued to ignore me, which was reassuring. Some of them fondled loose branches as if they were weapons, but they were not violent. Besides, I am my own dog.

They talked dialect and I stared at the flames. Cracklings popping over our heads felt like fireworks. In the distance we heard the idle din of the party.

I reached for a new sensation. I reached out to touch a walrus' cheek, and that started the fight. I got a kick in the stomach, and as I lay there looking at the night a pack of bikers drinking in the fields swooped down to kick the shit out of the Greenlanders.

Before I could get up I passed out. The next thing I know was a biker dragging me away before the Uro came. He said one of the Greenlanders was dead.

The ice ridges of the fields ripped open my back. The biker said I was leaving a trail of blood, and he cursed me.

Lights filled the field and he dropped me.

I fell into my darkness.

four

I am lying in a city hospital bed, letting my stitches rest. A policeman occupies a nearby chair. When I go to the toilet, he goes, too.

They found several hundred grams of hash while undressing me. I am to be deported as soon as I can be transported. I get to choose which border. They have no knowledge of my homeland, because I ditched my passport and I refuse to speak.

The ceiling is false cork and white. Counting all the pockmarks is like trying to count the stars. The ceiling has twelve different subsections over each bed. Each subsection contains hundreds of pockmarks. Each pockmark is one more hole in the universe.

They say I am malnourished. It is all the Full Moon Punch going to my liver, never stopping at my stomach to fill it up.

I have lain here too long without visitors. All civilized people have visitors.

"Do you play cards?" I ask the policeman.

"Don't tempt me." He sneers through a mound of facial hair.

"May I borrow your newspaper?"

"You're tempting me." He rises from his chair.

Already I can feel his club working up and down my legs, sweat pouring from his brow, a tight smile on his beard.

"Go ahead," I say. A warm chord runs through me. I will piss myself if he does.

But a group of policemen enter the ward. They are grinning. One waves a small packet. Terrible news. They have unearthed my passport.

I belong to an important country. I have a passport like a credit card. All the other countries accept it.

I am in Hamburg in the Hafenviertel. Hamburg is a nice place once you get beyond the train station. Maurice, a vagabond from France, cuts my hair. I have already shaved three times today. My train leaves in four hours for Copenhagen.

"Don't lose my identity," I urge Maurice as he clips away.

He shrugs. "Isn't that the purpose?"

I ask him to come with me. He refuses. Sometimes the whores from the Rapierbahn come down and give him a free one. Hamburg makes him very happy, he says.

"Except the train station," I laugh.

"The train station," Maurice looks at me gravely, "is the best part."

He takes me to the Hauptbahnhof. We descend secret stairways to a murky canal. Beneath the tracks, old men are racing swans. Their feathers gleam through the sludge.

"Care to bet," an Englishman asks.

"Never gamble," I say. I place five marks on number nine, Riding Hood.

Riding Hood wins. I give it all to Maurice. We dash back up the stairs and I make the moving train.

Good-bye Maurice.

How many times have I sat on a train approaching a border, queasy and tense with the fear of being detected? This time, however, I am my own illegal baggage. I do not want to go to jail, but I cannot be away from Christiania. So I take this risk. They need only to computer-check me to find out.

First the Germans. They look at me and see my passport and nod and grimace and generally act like idiots. But the walkie-talkies hooked on their belts remain unused.

Here come the Danes. They are big boys in their black winter coats. Why do so many Danes wear beards? Maybe they are trying to hide something from themselves.

I feel myself giving way. I want to shout, Take me, take me, just let's get it over with. My tongue flaps inside my mouth, my asshole puckers out to kiss the seat cushion.

The hairy Dane fondles my passport. His bulk fills the compartment door, and I have no place to flee.

Then I think of Otto. This always brings me calm. My hands rest on my knees, seeping sweat. The scarf around my neck weighs like a sacred cloak. Otto has come to me, to save me. My head is as light as a snowflake, and flurries off my shoulder to the window, to regard the Danish countryside in all its boring splendor.

The fucking Dane stamps my passport. I am free, free forever, free until caught again, free as no man can be, free like the snow in the air.

I am in Denmark.

five

Nothing has changed, and yet everything has. The Big Man says,

"Back again? You'll get caught."

Otto, my love, big all-powerful Otto, roars,

"Adam From Your Rib Jesus."

You missed a good Christmas party, someone says. We would have come visit you if we had known which hospital, another says.

Did you have a nice vacation, a third wants to know.

I will tell you who I am if you will tell me who I'm not.

There is a war going on. It is a war of words among people who own no dictionaries. The anarchists are fighting the pushers. Again.

Otto and I are on the sidelines, cheering.

"Fruits Poisons Serpents," Otto says.

They try to hold a discussion in Circus Hall. The seats are filled by serious-looking people. Kids play in the sandy floor imported from Dragor.

Points are raised but nobody can hear the mediator. The fighters throw sand at each other. The meeting spills outside. Everyone is packing snowballs. Women and children split on loyalties. It is a matter of principle. Either you want an ideal society prohibiting pushers, or you want a decadent society where everyone can support themselves.

Otto and I root for both sides. Always, the outcome is the same. The status quo wins. My job is saved. And the Big Man keeps his whale of a house.

But this time he holds a victory party.

Otto and I are to be the doormen.

Our instructions are simple. We make sure that anyone passing the whale enters it.

The whale is full of plastic chandeliers. Joints of the cheapest marijuana lie in circles on tin ashtrays. There are no chairs, only raw carpet and elevated bars. The Big Man's bartenders serve one drink, vin chaud made with homegrown red wine and brown sugar.

As people pass on the street we call out to them, "Party! Party!" like towncriers calling out the time. Only the invited dare to enter.

But we work on mescaline and earn our keep. Otto and I engage a fishing net, and we entrap the unwilling. Once inside, they debauche readily enough. It is only a matter of getting them inside, stringing them in like the spiders we are, to be devoured by our Big Man's party.

Activists dressed like pushers—leather jacketed and blue jeaned—stroll by, casing the whale. We snare them with the net. They do not try to escape. Otto rains them with religious cursewords: Moses and Jesus and God-damn.

We fling them through the doorway and they slink off to the nearest untouched ashtray.

The Big Man comes with more mescaline.

"No, thanks," I say.

"Are you sick?" He twiddles a fat marijuana cigar, letting it burn wastefully.

"Adam Vision Eve," Otto says.

"Horny?" I nod. "Want a whore?" the Big Man asks. I refuse. No more painted night shadows for me. The Big Man disapproves, retreats back into his whale.

I love you, I want to tell Otto. But I don't.

We wake up many days later on the doorstep, in mantels of snow. I run a fever around the block. Otto, too.

We shower in the whale, separately. Otto bellows an Italian operetto he has recently composed. The Big Man, thinking fast, tries to record it. But his Walkman recorder stereo cassette television video deck is jammed. Too bad. Otto never remembers anything he creates more than once.

We return to Christiania. It is full winter. Dogs have sprayed yellow on the fresh snow. On Pusher Street my colleagues have erected portable pot belly stoves that require only five men to move. Smoke columns from all the chimneys, and people steal wood from one another.

I take Otto home with me. He is too tired to resist. All the sleep wore him out.

I live in the Magic Forest, on Ostrich Lake. The lake is only a frozen belt of Christiania's canal. I have no neighbors, I live so deep in the woods.

My little home has two stories, but only one ceiling. The top floor belongs to the forest and the ground floor belongs to me. In the summer the forest spreads its vines all over its floor, mingling and sunbathing and sleeping if it is allowed to.

But in the winter the forest keeps away. It strains up into the sky, looking for warmth, because warm air rises. I do not even see the forest in the winter, it is so far up.

My ground floor is wood and brick and nude rock. My life's possessions are a tapestry, a table and a wooden chest for memories, when I have them or when I need them.

The mattress is an old friend's who left me a long time ago, and who I never think about. The old friend is God. God gave me the mattress when he was in Copenhagen one day. It is shaped like God's hand, and I lie on it whenever I get the chance.

All right. I stole the mattress. But no one misses it. Except me, when I'm not on it.

Otto disappears while I am trying to get in touch with myself. This is a long process that could take years, but I cheat so usually it takes only a few hours.

I do it sitting on the wooden chest, with the memories coming up and out my ass at once. All the memories touch each other on the way between here and there, commingling like customers in a revolving door, and that is how I get in touch with myself.

Often, while trying to get in touch with myself, I fall asleep. This time, too. All acts of revelation are short-lived, even stunted. You can choke yourself for only so long.

I find Otto outside of Christiania, just across the street. He is in Christianshavn Church, rolling around the pews, annoying no one because the church is empty.

"Otto," I croak.

He looks at me as if he doesn't recognize me. He is a big man turning a child's somersaults.

"Let's go upstairs," I say.

We start climbing the stairs. There must be thousands of them. First they are marble and user-worn. Then they are wood and creak beneath us. We ascend past the bells, big as milktrucks, and go outside. Now the steps have a verdigris coating, as they wind around the outside of the tower. It's freezing and I'm afraid to look down. But Otto does and I follow him.

Down below, across the street, for as far as we can see, stretches Christiania. It is so different from the city: all brown and muddy, with bonfires and melting snowmen everywhere. No streets. No cars. Just people and naked trees and buildings that only isolates or socialists could live in, half crumbling with mud trailing up their entries.

"Let's go down," I ask Otto. The height makes me dizzy, and the wind has frozen my nose snot. I clutch the railing at every step. Otto lags behind me, roaring at the wind.

At the bottom of the stairway, thousands of steps down, is a plaque. It honors the architect who designed the church a couple centuries ago. It says he killed himself because the spiral stairway around the tower ran the wrong way.

We go to Moonfisher to drink. It is too cold to stay outside, so we have to sit at the bar. A chandelier hangs from an aqua blue ceiling. Paper moons perch on top of green candy-striped poles. Otto drinks on credit. I have to pay immediately.

At sunset the chandelier goes on, is dimmed. Blinking lights race around the bar's mirrored backing, rushing through Chinese parasols at the mirror's corners. Dogs are beginning to fill the place. The bartenders, whose faces I know but whose names I don't, dish up shot glasses full of jelly beans and malted milk balls.

I fill a chillum and Otto and I smoke. Various scavengers come begging for a hit. Otto growls at them. The in-people at the bar and the center table talk their in-people nonsense: art and politics.

After a while people begin to pass out. A Greenlander lies face down on a table at the door. Some tourists stoned in a remote corner have fallen asleep, drooling.

Otto disappears with a silver-haired shrew, and now I am alone. I start searching for a woman. It's never easy: looking for the look that looks back. Even in Christiania, which is supposed to have free sex, it is difficult. Four men for every woman here, I think. Like a cowboy town.

Today I sold half a kilo. The Big Man gave me a hot dog with all the trimmings, he was so happy. No one sells half a kilo on a February day. But I did. I am a shoo-in for Pusher of the Month.

I go alone to one of Christiania's music clubs for a celebration. Even in full winter the tourists overrun the place. Johnny Vampire and the Vomiteers are playing.

>Baby, I don't wanna be
>your percolator
>Just wanna be
>your masturbator
>Do me til I glow
>I'll make you til you flow
>Oh-oh-oh!

The tourists dance like wounded pigeons. They all seem to know each other. Boys who smile at rivals through a fog of smoke. Girls who are good at asking you questions about yourself, but incapable of listening to your answers...

Otto never comes here, so I don't know what I'm doing here. I leave.

The night is Scandinavia, white clouds scuttling across a black velveteen sky. I look at it for a long time, then surrender to the pull of the Magic Forest.

On Ostrich Lake some people are skating. Their blades crossing the ice make sounds like the slow sharpening of a knife. I lie on my ground floor, listening to them and fearing for them, fearing for the ice, worrying about people and things I do not know.

It is times like this that I realize I am doing Otto's thinking. These thoughts cannot be my own. They are Otto's, but he is sleeping and can't do them, so I do them for him. I love him that much.

In our garden there are serpents and fruits and two people, one coming from the other coming from me. They live in a state of undeclared war, like we all do. Everything that happens is a secret, and you don't know about it, even if it happens to you.

six

I have great pains in my chest, near my breasts. At intervals they are stabbing pains, but mostly it is the dull throb of a sour bone.

I tell myself it is my ulcer moving up.

I eat bananas and beer every meal to quell the ache, but it doesn't help. I smoke joints, aspirate nitrous oxide, eat antacid. Nothing works.

I tell Otto and he laughs. But says nothing! Something's going on. Otto knows. I know he knows.

All the bananas and beer are hurting my stomach. I switch to milk, in hope of coating my insides.

My stomach fascinates me. It is something I will never see. I think it must look like a man from outerspace: the intestines are his tail and the actual stomach is his face.

I am losing weight. My diet makes me shit yellow turds. The pain in my chest goes all up and down my ribs.

Heartburn, I tell myself. Otto knows better. He eats lollipops now to suckle his secret knowledge. He grins all the time, Otto does. He looks almost relieved.

The Big Man yells at me. My sales are falling. My customers all think me ill and won't touch my merchandise. I try to reassure them by saying I have cancer. But that seems only to confirm their worst suspicions.

Right now I just can't sell.

I go to the bakery every day for a handout. I force down their wretched bread that looks so nice because I want to live. Because.

The people at the bakery remind me of the end of the world. They all look familiar—as if out of a dream or deja vu—but I know none of them personally.

Surrender. I will go to the Christiania Health House. I have never been there before. But I am so sick. I feel like I am going to have a baby.

The problem, I think, is spring. The sky moves so fast I cannot keep track of it. That causes me pain. In one day there can be snow, then rain, then sun, then snow again, and finally a clear black night. It is like living on the screen of a kaleidoscope.

Candles lay on all the tables and windowsills of the Health House. It felt like a funeral home. The advice, given by one of those Irish who drive priests away, was to come again, when someone more qualified is on the job. Preferably a Friday afternoon. I will not come again.

The pain does not fade. The intervals between stabs grow shorter.

It's half spring, spring like a thousand seasons.

"Good news," the Big Man says. "A shipment of Lebanon. Your problems are over."

"How?" I want to know.

"Everybody buys Lebanon. You'll start to sell again."

I turn away. I do not want to sell again. I want to get well. The pain has caused a tic. My left nostril flares without warning. I will be a laughing stock.

The Big Man comes to visit me at night. He is trying to save me.

"Look what I brought." He pulls out a kilo of Lebanon. It looks like a chunk of tar, black and sticky. He puts it by my head, then sits on my memory chest.

"Smoke some," he urges. He tosses a chillum at me.

I grind off pieces to fluffy bits, and begin to smoke. I inhale chillum after chillum after chillum. Hours pass. Soon it will be sunrise. I am floating up to meet it. A grin like a worm spreads across the Big Man's face. Pain stabs my ribs.

"All right." I forget what it is I want to say. "I'll sell today."

I am standing at a table on the Street. The sun shines. For the moment. I have sold three hundred grams and it is not even noontime.

Then the siren goes and it is noon. All around me the pushers' dogs and activists' dogs and tourists' dogs and unaffiliated dogs imitate the caterwaul, their long narrow noses and hairy phlegmy jaws pointed to the sky as if they all expect to be borne away.

I look over and she is standing before me like an apparition.

"I am Luna," she whispers.

Her hair lies as white as the moon, and she has a moon-shaped face. I look at her. My eyes tear.

"Give me your troubles," she whispers. "And I will eat them."

Her nose runs, and spittle dribbles from the corners of her mouth. Her eyes give a blank wild stare, like a silent shriek—as if she sees something I cannot see, something monstrous.

She takes shallow breaths. I am watching her. Her shrieking eyes widen imperceptibly, her skin grows paler, almost cadaver-like, so her blue veins shine like trip-lines on her arms and legs. She is beautiful, she is translucent. She is Luna. And she is the moon.

I hustle her off of Pusher Street. We are behind buildings now, in a courtyard of mud and dogshit, clutching each other uncertainly by the forearms.

"Are you real?" I finally ask her.

She refuses to talk except in whispers. "I am Luna."

I am thinking drugs. I am thinking I have done so many of them that I cannot separate fantasy from reality. I am thinking illusion.

I pinch her and she squirms, but makes no effort to escape or dissolve or whatever apparitions do.

I crush her to me. She smells of mildew and animals.

"Give me your troubles," she whispers again. "And I will eat them."

The pain in my ribs has vanished.

I take her to the Bathhouse. When she sees the dripping white tiles and the foamy white bodies, her eyes shriek like sirens.

I peel off my clothes. She follows. I pretend not to look at her. Her body is chalk white, a little wide at the hips like a fine vase, with drooping breasts and sooted knees.

Steam gathers in clouds on the ceiling and at the window. At the far end several tattooed bodies hide their faces in thick sprays of water.

Luna stands under the shower as if expecting judgment. I turn the faucet and out pours the water. Her mouth opens but no sound comes. She stands there, her arms held out stiffly from her sides.

I rub a bar of soap down her back. She remains still, her mouth open. I cannot help myself. My soapy fingers wander to bellybutton and breasts and nipples. Yet she stands rigidly. I begin to feel guilty. I wash her, then myself.

In the dressing room I have to dry her. She refuses to do anything herself. She says nothing. Her eyes are filled with the same sightless horror.

She does everything by me steering her, like a blind person.

It is night time and we lie on my mattress in the forest. I fight myself about sleeping with her. She is truly sick, mentally sick.

Aren't we all?

I climb on top of her. She grabs me and draws me inside, her eyes still wide, her breathing deep. She digs her fingernails into my back, and tugs my shoulders until I am pressing against her breasts.

I am so happy I begin to cry. Then I feel guilty and grow soft.

I roll off her. Through the dark her shrieking eyes glow like mirrors. "What do you see?" I finally ask her.

"I see the vanity of the world," she whispers.

Today we go looking for Otto. He is not hard to find. We have only to listen carefully.

She approaches him like she already knows him, a smile on her lips. They whisper together a few minutes. Otto whispering! When they are done they beckon me to join them. I try to swagger, but it is more like a stagger.

They say nothing. Otto strokes his beard. I feel short. I stand next to my lover and my infatuation, and I am scared.

Finally they start to walk and I walk with them. We go into the Magic Forest. Our shoes crunch the snow. The trees are black and a moon hangs in the cloudless day sky.

We pass my home but make no effort to stop. We walk far along the river. Here, in the cold stagnant swamps, squat pieces of homes that were never completed.

Finally, we come to a group of people gathered around a fire. Everyone says hello to each other. There are several mutilees among the throng.

"Watch out!" a midget warns me. "We're all crazy."

Otto knocks Luna and me together and grins and roars something maybe in Latin.

The crowd cheers. Most of them have Irish accents. Their faces are dirty but friendly. Two bottles of whiskey are passed. Luna kisses everybody. A gaggle of cats fights over a deep basin of whiskied milk.

"How was the ceremony?" an old man in a woolly sweater asks.

Otto claps his hands and roars some more. Greek? They all laugh. Luna sits down in the circle around the fire. I follow. When the whiskey comes my way, I take two violent tugs and pass it on.

We stay there for the rest of the day. The Irish tell each other stories. Often there are silent moments so comfortable that nobody feels obliged to speak. At darkness the gathering breaks. Everybody nods at each other like worshippers leaving a Sunday church service.

Otto leads us out to the cobblestone plaza. He kisses Luna good-night and then he puts his lips to mine and I taste the salt and the sea and the earth and the stars, I taste the colors purple and gold and green, I taste rocks and stones and diamond and emerald and jade. He kisses me good-night on the lips and I taste everything. He stumbles back to his hammock, and I trace my finger over my lips for a long time. Finally, Luna leads me back into the forest.

seven

Our life together. We never talk. I use my voice only to sell hash.

We lie down a lot. All of us are touching. Our knees converse when we make love. Our tongues rummage in each other's mouths. Every day is the height of spring.

But her eyes still shriek and maybe I can never change them.

I wonder a lot about the duty of a lover. Provide, protect, support, cherish? Can I do all these things? Does she even love me?

We go for long walks in the forest. It helps to air out her mildew smell. Her yellow strings of hair grow longer, her face widens to a Luna-moon.

Otto and the Big Man like to sit with us for hours. The Big Man doesn't say anything either. We sit without words. But we drink. Sometimes I want to stand up and sing, or shout. Something to mark my presence. But I don't. We are all too content.

When we aren't selling hash, Luna decides where we go and what we do. I follow her everywhere. She is my salvation. She is nearly replacing Otto as my religion.

The Big Man is very happy.

"You get married. You settle down. You sell better," he says. He grows a little belly with my sales. I am happy for him. He is happy for me. Everybody is happy for everyone.

Sometimes Luna will whisper something in my ear, and I am beyond happy. I soar. She whispers only phrases.

They might be biblical.

"Enter me my flock," she whispers. And I do.

I want to ask her questions but I am not sure she can speak in dialogue. So sometimes I just monologue. And once or twice she whispers her phrases. "The world and they that dwell therein," she whispers.

I would like to take her dancing but she doesn't dance. I'd like to take her out to dinner but she gets dizzy in restaurants. Flowers, jewelry, candy—all the accoutrements of love have no appeal to her.

I want to write her poetry. But Otto is our poet, and there can be only one poet in a circle of friends.

So our love is a silent love, its only expression sexual.

I am beginning to think that silence is the true form of happiness, that conversations made of pauses are dialogues filled with happiness, that happiness is what happiness gets.

And falling in love? Falling in love and silence are two interdependent acts. You cannot be loud when you are in love. The only love is a mutual silence. I am trying so hard to hold it.

It is summer, but Luna is a winter person. Pallor and moon-faces and silence are not meant for the shirtless summer crowds, in which people gather outside to fill the sky with their noise. Summer is for talkers. We stay out in the forest, fending off the flies, listening to the workings of our stomachs. Otto's growls, mine whirs, Luna's says nothing.

She is the Queen of Quietness, the Princess of Pinfall, the Duchess of Dumbness, the Lady of Lull, the Woman of Whist.

We do our wash in the canal, then hang it on a clothesline outside our home. The long-sleeved shirts droop like so many Christs and Otto claps in approval.

Business, too, goes well. The tourists with their half-shut suspicious eyes are easy to cheat. They are mostly Danes and Germans and Americans, crawling about the place like lice in a shock of hair. You can tell them by their daypacks, little bags full of paraphernalia and clothes and food. The Americans tie sweaters around their waists as if expecting the Ice Age. The Germans haven't learned to shave yet. And the Danes, at home but not at home, point and gawk and cackle like children at a zoo. Sometimes, too, there are some groovies up from Amsterdam wondering what all the commotion is about. They leave disappointed.

eight

Conversation. I can't take it anymore. The pure form of communication, the natural form, is monologue.

Today the Big Man told me something, then I told him something, then him again, then we stopped. Silence. If we heard each other we agreed on many points. Maybe.

"If you sell well, then you are happy and I am happy," the Big Man said.

"Birds make too much noise in the summer," I said.

"We have twenty more kilos of Lebanon and fifteen more kilos of Moroccan to sell. Then we'll all take a vacation together," said the Big Man.

After that, we had our slice of silence. We agreed. It is the people who never agree who talk all the time, fill their silence with arguments and indiscretions. Conversations are not accords. They are word fights, people packing up their words tight into wordballs and throwing them at each other.

Luna and I never talk. That means we agree all the time, which means we are in love.

If all books had blank pages, then literature would be a form of happiness. But books are harangues and paintings are harangues and conversations are harangues and rock songs are harangues. Art is harangue.

Otto and I break into the bakery. We are stealing bread for our vacation picnic with the Big Man. Otto goes for the dark heavy stuff—rye bread and honey salt and grahams loaves as fat and flat as a dead man's feet. I prefer the light white junk—french bread and wienerbrod with the icing scraped off and flutes, scores of flutes tied up like faggots.

We hear the bakers coming and slip through the front window.

The Big Man is waiting with a long purple sausage. Luna carries a basket full of red tomatoes and green heads of lettuce.

We climb into the Big Man's Alfa Romeo and head for Dragor, past all the ugly city people with their quizzical faces and talking minds, always talking.

The fishing village holds groups of old men scratching their balls and chewing cigars, gazing over their green-mouthed Carlsberg bottles at each other, trying to pass the time. Into a public library file an army of old women, clacking their dentures in anticipation. Otto roars in Greek or Latin and the women dive through the door into the mice den of books and newspapers and funnies. Old people in the summer.

At the beach we can't find a square of sand without someone's tape deck blaring in our ears. Otto goes to work. He roars and shrieks and exposes himself and farts and takes a whiz. In ten minutes the beach is ours, the silent beach.

We watch the sun. It moves too fast. First in your eyes, then at your head and soon over your shoulders. There is nothing you can do about it. The old men in the village cheer it on, waiting to join it up there in the sky, so far away in the dark that you can't even see it.

Luna hides her face in a veil and wraps her body in muslin cloth. Otto slices rents in his tweed overcoat for ventilation. The Big Man lounges in a zoot suit, rubbing his sideburns with lemon juice.

I sleep. When I awake the sun is still there, waiting to come down into the town and burn its buildings into orange. Otto is cleaning his nails with a sand crab's claw. Further away than he need be, the Big Man squats in the sand, relieving his lunch. Luna is gazing at the pale blue twilight sky, full of nothing like the richest silence you can imagine, full of possibilities.

We stop at a Grill Bar for dinner. Otto and the Big Man have roasted chicken. I order a Maxi-Burger. Luna sips a chocolate milk.

We spend the night in the Big Man's whale, sucking on his wrinkled joints. No one speaks and everyone is listening. The Big Man says good-night.

Good-night, Big Man.

nine

I do not understand these woman things.

Luna shrieks and shrieks, my silent Luna. In the morning her head is bent low over her knees, spewing yesterday's food. She moans and weeps and wails, I don't know what.

I am stupid. She is pregnant, with child, in the family way, breeding, teeming, parturient. Expecting. Oh God. Oh Otto.

This is a bad time. I return to the Health House, like a peasant to the great knowledgeable village doctor.

"My Luna is pregnant," I say.

"Congratulations."

"We don't want the child," I say. "An abortion..."

"Why not have the child? An abortion will be very expensive. It will take years before her insides will be the same—"

"We want an abortion," I say in my lowest, most humble way.

"You want murder," he says, a Dane with a beard.

I think of all the dirty brats running around Christiania, all the—

"You must take responsibility for your actions," that voice of his drones on, the voice of knowledge and authority that has never known the truth of silence.

"Children are very nice," he also says. He pats me on

the back.

"Have the child," he says.

I tug his beard to my face. I am almost violent. I spell it out for him. "We want an abortion," I say so close to him my lips touch his beard, a beard like a scouring brush.

"Okay," he says. "Take it easy. Of course you can have one. But it will cost you."

"How much?"

"More than you have. Besides, is your Luna a Danish citizen? Of course not. The local hospital authorities will have to approve it. You must talk to them."

I leave him in his wake of words. I get some change and find a phone, dial the Copenhagen Social Consideration Center.

A woman answers the phone. She sounds nice enough. I explain my side, she explains hers. Luna must be interviewed and approved. The value of her to Denmark will be considered.

"You have a 50-50 chance, I would guess," says the woman on the phone.

I hang up. My beautiful Luna doesn't even talk. How will she ever interview?

Back in my little home, where the walls have always been crumbling but seem more smoldering now, Luna paces. Sometimes she beats the walls with her white, bony fists. She is always shrieking, frightening the trees in a voice they've never heard. She begins to talk, streams of words in Swedish that I can't understand.

Otto comes. Together they make a sound like mating elephants, trembling and sonorous. They are not agreeing on anything. They are talking.

Who wants this child? Not I, to see my Luna's belly stretched big and tight like a saxophonist's billowing cheeks. A child will kill her. Many more women die in childbirth than anyone is willing to admit. There is a worldwide conspiracy to suppress this information because reproduction is viewed as essential to the survival of our race.

So I am lying. But it could be true. Anything has an element of truth because anything can happen. Anything.

I go to the Big Man to ask his advice. "Luna is pregnant," I say.

"Too bad." He shakes his head and tweaks his nose. "This isn't the right time for you."

"Not at all," I agree.

"What are you going to do about it?"

"Abort."

"Abort? Where, back in Sweden? You know she can't go back there. They'd lock her up in a minute."

I begin to list possibilities, all the great cities with fine names. Amsterdam, London, Paris. The Big Man shrugs.

"Go anyplace. Do anything," he says. "Do what Luna wants."

ten

I return to Luna. She sits there with a smile on her face like an iced herring.

"Luna," I say. "Luna."

She stares at me with her frozen grin.

"Say something," I say. "Anything."

"I have gotten a man with help," she whispers.

The Big Man comes. "Pull yourself together," he says to Luna. He pats her on the shoulder. She shrinks from his touch, smiling.

He turns to me. "Amsterdam," he says. "Maybe Amsterdam. I can lend you the money."

"Thanks," I say.

"You know," he says. "She'll never make it."

"I know."

"Maybe if you went into the interview with her and explained—"

"Explained what?"

"Everything," he says, his arm sweeping the house like a magic wand.

I call the Social Consideration Center again. The same lady answers.

"I want to set up an interview for my girlfriend," I say.

"Okay," she says. "Meet me here tomorrow morning. We'll have a talk."

My girlfriend can't talk, I want to say. But I don't.

Down white corridors on white floors we move, Luna and I. All the doors have numbers on them, and nameplates and doorknobs. We find the right number with matching nameplate. I have Luna by the arm. I knock.

"Come in," calls the lady.

We enter. All the furniture is Danish—black and metal and elegantly simple, like a torture chamber. A pair of shoes step forward. A hand comes out.

"I am Lise Sorensen," she says.

I look at the hand a minute. It is too white and all dried up from many soapings. Then, "This is Luna," I say.

"Pleased to meet you," Lise Sorensen says. The hand goes away. Our feet face each other on the white floor.

"Won't you sit down," Lise Sorensen says. She gestures to a pair of angry chairs. I guide Luna to one of them, and help her in. She sits carefully, tucking her feet up beneath her body. The chair shudders, but stays upright.

I go to my chair. It is two pieces of black plastic molded onto a metal frame. Famous Danish furniture. I sit down.

"Now," says Lise Sorensen. She smiles. "How should we begin?"

"I don't know," I say. "We need an abortion."

"Why?"

"Because Luna's pregnant and we don't want the

child."

"Why not?" Lise Sorensen smiles.

"We're too young."

Lise Sorensen laughs. "You both must be at least thirty," she says.

"We're still too young," I say.

"Luna?" says Lise Sorensen.

Luna rolls her head a little bit, as if to knock around her brain.

"Luna?" Lise Sorensen says again.

Luna puts her fingers to her lips, wets them, and puts them back down on her knee.

"Luna doesn't talk," I say.

"Why not?"

Why, why not, why, why not—I wonder when this is going to end.

"Because of her religion," I say. "She's a devout anarchist. They're not allowed to talk."

"I see." Lise Sorensen smiles. "Like a monk."

"So can we have the abortion?"

"It depends. How long have you two been in Denmark?"

"Three years," I say.

"Legally?" I shake my head. "Where do you live?"

"Christiania."

"What do you do for a living?"

"Bake bread," I lie. "How much longer is this going to last?"

"I don't know. How badly do you want the abortion?"

I look into her face for the first time. It is a face as empty as a frozen sea, but it is not unfriendly.

"I want it very much," I say. "I want..."

"Yes?"

I am so tired. "I want to live and be happy, not just live, but to really feel life, to be free and feel life like the wind against my face. And I want to love and soar with it, not just have it bellyflop down all the time. I want to feel like a bird, not a sailboat. That's what I want."

I don't know what happened. I am standing up, gripping her strange white formica desk, shouting into her face. How did I get here?

"I think that's enough." The woman stands up to face me. "We'll let you know."

We are out on the street. The gray drab city street with traffic lights and cars and newspaper headlines screaming stuff from Iraq and Lebanon and the United States. We are arm-in-arm on the street. I am too tired to walk any more. I need a drink.

There is a pub to the right. We go in. Everyone stops talking. We go out again and I am no longer too tired to walk.

eleven

Waiting for the mail. I have not received a letter in years. The last one was

Remember. We live in the present. The past does not matter and the future does not exist, or vice-versa.

The Big Man waits with us.

"They'll never approve it," he says. "Why'd you lose control?"

"I was tired," I say. "I am like that."

"Sometimes I don't know why I bother with any of you," he says. "Is it for the money? Of course it's for the money. I love to make money. But why with such fuck-ups? If I wanted I could go to Amsterdam and everything would be more standardized there. You know what I'm saying? I wouldn't have to deal with pregnant women who can't talk, with castabouts who lose control at the drop of a glove, with all these dogs. It would be normal, I think, in Amsterdam."

"What is normal?" I ask.

"Don't give me that rhetorical crap. I'm normal, that's what's normal. I'm the only normal one here, and I don't even live here."

"I know," I say.

"Beauty in the eye of the Beholder," Luna whispers. "And they sin."

The Big Man falls silent, thinking about that.

I look around. The house is a mess, unused tampons all over the place, the tapestry dangling halfway off the wall. In the silence everyone examines their hands. Luna's knees press up against her chest. The Big Man grips a chunk of hash.

I hear the tourists swimming in Ostrich Lake. They are naked and happy and full of wonder at the freedom here. Even some Christianians swim naked in the lake, though I have never done it. I hear them all splashing and laughing and undressing and dressing again, the shuffle of buckles and shoes and shirts. The summer crowd.

"Let's find Otto and go to Dragor," I say.

"It won't be the same," the Big Man says.

"I don't want to just sit here and wait," I say.

"You have to." He gets up. "I'm going to take a look at business," he says. "I'll be back."

Luna and I alone now. Look in my eyes, Luna. See how I love you and how happy and confused you make me. See how I think of you all the time and I feel you all over always. See me, Luna? I am here and so are you. We are here together.

Rolph the Mailman comes.

"Letter for you, Luna," he says, smiling. Everyone in the summer is so damn happy.

Luna sits there ignoring him. I take the letter. Rolph remains, curious.

"Go away, Rolph," I say.

"You're so paranoid," he says. And leaves.

I turn to Luna. "You want to open it?" She clutches her knees to her chin. I open it. It's a short letter. We can't help you, it says.

Good luck, it says. Best wishes, too.

Luna reads my face, shrieks until the tapestry falls down. Then she is silent. For a moment even the swimmers stop splashing. Then life resumes.

"I'm so sorry," I say. I move to touch her. She cowers.

"We can go to Amsterdam," I say.

She looks at me for a second, her eyes swirling like snails. Then she bolts up and is past me before I can stop her.

"Luna," I scream. "Luna."

I have a flashlight and Otto has a voice and the Big Man has a mind.

"Moon," Otto roars. "Moon, moon, moon."

"Where could she be?" the Big Man says. "Who does she know?"

"Everywhere," I say. "Everyone."

We start on the far side of Ostrich Lake, exploring the potato farms. "Would you like a drink?" an Irish asks.

"No time," says the Big Man. "We're looking for Luna."

"Luna who?"

"Silent Luna."

"I see," the Irish says. "What did she steal?"

"Nothing, you idiot. We're worried that she's lost her

way."

"Hey," the Irish says. "Let it happen. Isn't that the way?"

"She's out of it," I say. "The Uro could pick her up. She might freeze to death."

"In the summer?"

"Imbecile Adam Eve Abel Cain," Otto roars.

"Shut up, Otto," the Irish says. "Do you want some help?"

"Sure," the Big Man says. "Why not."

The Irish goes away, comes back again, now with four friends and two bottles. "Might as well make it a party," the Irish says.

"Might as well," the Big Man sighs. We clomp through the potatoed soil, everyone calling, "Luna, Luna." But no answer, the bottle passing back and forth.

From the potato farm we stumble to the carrot collective.

"What's going on there?" a voice calls.

"It's us, German Thomas," the Irishman named Dan yells back. "We're looking for Silent Luna. She's missing."

"Be right out," German Thomas says. He comes with several others, bearing torches like in old movies. Everyone calls Luna, and drinks and smokes. In the torchlight the faces are all sealed and flushed, as if sunburnt.

"Quite a party," says German Thomas.

"We should do this more often," Dan replies.

The alcohol and smoke nearly swallow my anxiety, but not quite. The torches light their faces and everyone is giggling.

At the strawberry collective a Norwegian girl calls out, "I thought the Solstice was last month."

"It's Luna. She's missing," says German Thomas.

"Missing? How exciting. We'll be right with you."

A troop of Nordic women emerge, wrapped in several shades of purple, wearing scarves and bandannas and kneewraps.

"I'm getting dizzy," I whisper to the Big Man.

"Take it easy," the Big Man says. "It's only other people."

"I know. Where's Otto?"

"Back eating strawberries."

"Otto," I call.

"I thought it was Luna," one of the women says.

"Maybe it's both," German Thomas answers. "Or maybe it's all of us. Maybe we're all lost."

"Too much," the woman says. "That's really too much."

"It feels like there are a hundred people," I say to the Big Man.

"Relax. There are only twenty."

"I can't take it," I say. And all the time we are walking. "Don't think about it."

At the canal they stop to confer.

"I think we should swim over," German Thomas suggests.

"Why?" the Big Man wants to know.

"We can search the water that way."

"All right!" Dan whistles.

"Too much," Riina giggles. "That's really too much."

They all jump in, clothes and everything, and wrestle their way across. The Big Man and I take the bridge.

"Fools," says the Big Man.

"I told you."

When they get out of the water I swear they have multiplied by five or six. But Otto has returned and I feel better.

"Red Sea in you Bush, Moses," Otto shouts. "Forty Days in Seven Hours."

"Somebody give him a drink," says German Thomas. "That should help."

At Pusher Street, empty now, some of them get down on their hands and knees to comb the uneven cobblestone.

"Luna, Luna," they moan.

The Big Man and I keep searching. It is almost daybreak. The sky glows an eerie metallic blue. We trudge over the humped fields, past the closed nightclubs with their doors chained shut, calling her name. We are all getting tired. The Big Man winds his head around his shoulders, trying to stay awake.

"Look!" he starts. "Up there."

I follow his arm to its finger to the top of Christianshavn Church. A figure made of mildew and the moon leans against the railing of the spiral staircase.

"Luna," I shriek. "Luna." The Germans and Norwegians and Irish come running.

"Wow," Dan says. "There she is."

She is there and I am here and I call her and if she hears me she does not show it.

"Luna," I scream. "Luna."

"Take it easy," the Big Man says, tugging at my forearm.

"Luna," he calls. "It's me. Why don't you come down?" We are directly beneath her now. The sky is breaking light everywhere, on the buildings and the sidewalks and the church's steeple. On Luna.

She gives a low piercing shriek like a kettle boiling. And then she soars.

"That's too much," Riina says. "That's really too much."

When people fall from high distances they do not break a lot on the outside. But they die.

twelve

The funeral. Everyone wears white. Eight five-year-olds are the pallbearers, caked in clown make-up. The Christiania Free Symphony plays:

> Where have you gone Luna Daisyland
> Your Mother Magic Helper could not cry
> Don't know why

The Big Man has bought me a beautiful cream suit with matching tophat.

"The husband of the suicide," people murmur.

The Big Man says his piece. "She lived too fast," he says. "But now she's finally getting her rest." Some people whistle and clap in approval. Others hiss.

"Too conventional," they say.

But it is all very fine.

They lower the casket into the ground and she is gone.

"Here's some money," the Big Man says, pushing me a wad of bills. "Consider it an advance. Now get out of here. Go to Spain or someplace like that. Take Otto for company."

"Thank you."

"Come back when it runs out, or when you're ready. Whichever comes first."

We take the train. I sedate Otto with twenty valium.

We find a compartment to ourselves, draw the corridor shades to keep people away. The Big Man stands on the platform, begins to wave. I wave back. We pull away, gather speed and are gone.

Otto snores. He sleeps all the way to Barcelona. I don't do anything but watch the countries pass. It soothes me. The train is so quick and capable, nothing ever happens on it, and yet you see all of life through your train window. You feel it, too. If only life could be lived from a train window, where you can experience everything and nothing at the same time. That would be nice.

But in Barcelona we get off and it is no longer nice. Dust in your eyes and dirt rings your mouth after a few minutes on the street. Otto growls and I have no more valium. I am thinking that an island would be nice but over water they all seem so far away.

"Moon, moon, moon," Otto begins to cry. We must get moving or we will cry together. A train to Malaga. Because it sounds like the name of a flower.

PART II

one

We have been here for a time. The sun shines thickly on the bluffs where we camp, above the waves, not far from the Old Town.

Otto is as brown and wrinkled as a walrus. I look good, too. The alcohol is cheap, it is really wonderful. People like us, too.

I go to a bar while Otto mingles with the gypsies. The gypsies are the pushers here, and late at night in the plaza they whisper at you, "Hash...hash," drawing out the word like a song.

I go to one bar in particular, small like a womb. An Englishman runs it, named Charley. He comes from Bath where he was a carpenter. His wife left him so he left England. He likes it here, in Torremolinos. His Spanish partner, who everyone calls Jay, is like a Brit, too, has the same taste for the sun and the women.

There are so many women at Charley's, it is dazzling. One night I was there very late, sipping San Miguel. I am always there very late. But this one night, five—six—women come in. I watch. They take a table on the plaza, and Charley and two others rush to them.

"Ahh, Senoritas," Charley says.

"Charley," these women screech. Everyone knows each other. Charley splashes out the cognac, gives me a swish, too.

Most of the women are dressed in white, to highlight their tans. Some are blonde, two are brunettes. They speak with different accents, but they know each other. The Spaniards wear black to match the night.

After several cognacs the Spaniards get up, two Spanish women. They touch backs to each other and clap their feet against the floor.

"Ole," Charley shouts.

They do a flamenco, I guess. I have seen the pictures many times in front of the nightclubs, these women in frilled skirts and tall hairstyles. But these are local, regular beautiful women in black satin pantsuits with freshwater pearls ringing their necks, reeling and clapping and stamping on a floor in a bar.

When they finish their eyes glow and their skin shines. Charley and the tenders stack chairs in a hurry, swoop down to escort the women onward. I wander out as they haul down the caged door to close off the place.

"See you tomorrow," I say to Charley.

"See you," he says.

That was one night.

Otto came back late and we sat and talked. He doesn't growl or roar anymore, he only rasps, like the scraping of loose gravel beneath your foot.

He still says the same things, but no one can understand him.

"Nomads Virgins Spaniards," he said that night.

"The same or different?" I asked.

But he had fallen asleep. He is still the most different person I have ever met.

Per likes him, too. Per is a Danish writer I met one night at Charley's—Charley's is all I ever go to. Per says Otto is profound.

"Do you love Otto?" Per asked yesterday.

"Of course."

"I had thought—"

"What?"

"Well, maybe—"

"What?"

"Never mind," Per said. He folded his hands in his lap, and sat there. Despite all the sun, he had a very pale face, and I studied it. He kept his hair short which made him seem younger, but his nose pinching his face sent lines around his mouth and beneath his eyes. In candle-light or near a mirror he seemed very old.

"Let's go to Charley's," I said.

"I can't."

"Why not?"

"I have a visitor coming," he said mysteriously. I left it at that.

The road that ascends from the beach up to the town is lined with pubs and leather shops. Every now and then there are steps to get you up more quickly. No cars are allowed—it is just a walking road.

On the left as you climb the shops disappear for a

moment, and all there is are the low red-tiled roofs of old homes. Crowds gather at the walls to watch, and as you edge closer you can see why. The cats: all bone and speckled black and white, mewling and lagging in the shade, hundreds of them perched on the roofs like out of some zoo scene. The tourists watch for several minutes, throw crumbs or coins that no cat would touch, and then climb onward, up into the main street where small department stores and fine cafes wrestle for their money.

One night I couldn't sleep. Otto snored beside me, the sky was thick with stars and from the town came a low happy aimless din. I slipped out of my sleeping bag and went for a walk.

The main walking road was shut down. All the pearls and cameras and leather bags were locked behind the caged storefronts, and over the heating shafts rolled a few sleepless drifters. The gypsies stayed to the plaza, and all the others got a slice of pavement on the pedestrian street.

Torremolinos seemed very mysterious to me then. Maybe I was falling in love with the world again. All the day glitter and night dirt drew me in its contrast, tugged at my heartstrings like something real and grotesque, something I could touch and feel.

I headed down the walking street, past all the stores in their cages, to where the shops fell away and the cats played. I looked over the wall and they were there, swarming in the night like locusts. I started to climb over the wall. It was a slight drop to the roof but if it could hold all those cats, it could hold me.

I slipped down to the roof and fell among the cats. They scratched at my clothes and pawed at my face. I felt their loose fur and ridged bones, and let them topple over me like I was some object in a playground. I lay on my face and felt them all over me. Overhead the moon glowed happy and free, and I felt one with it.

two

The next days, weeks were very good to us. Charley spotted me beers in his bar, and the gypsies gave Otto chunks of hash to bring home. In mid fall, the tourist population began to dwindle. The only ones left were the very rich and the very poor. The contrast inspired me, and I spent hours without anxiety of any kind.

Per acted strange, though. He blushed every time we met, and when we had dinner together, he got stuck in the middle of sentences, drowned in his thoughts.

"What's the matter?" I finally asked.

"Something's happening," he whispered.

"Yes?"

"My life, it's just not...thing's aren't...well, I've stopped..." and his voice trailed off like a radio losing its batteries.

Charley came by and gave Per a pat on the back. "See you boys at the bar later?"

"As always," I said.

"As always," Per sighed. Charley drifted off. "How well do you know him?" Per whispered.

"He pours my beer every night." I shrugged. "Not much." The simple clarity in which I now held life receded every time I talked with Per, and it bothered me. I took a long swallow of beer and yawned.

"You make life seem so violent," I finally said. "And

it isn't. At least, not here."

"You're so blind," Per bleated. "You've done too many drugs."

"I guess so. Come on." I got up. "Let's go to Charley's."

The television showed a good football game, and the bar was crowded with the usual mix of Spaniards and Brits. I felt happy and drank heavily. But every time I turned around Per was glaring at Jay and Charley.

I elbowed Per. "Stop being so weird," I said.

He grabbed me by the arm. "Listen," he said.

I tried to, but my eyes wandered back to the screen.

"I'm scared," Per said.

"So am I. Try not to think about it."

"We're not scared of the same things," he whispered.

"I don't think this is the place to talk about it."

"Okay," he said. "We'll talk later. Maybe we'll go for a walk when the game is over."

"Maybe."

The game ended but I made Per stay while I watched the women. They always seemed to be different women, and it was hard to figure out where Charley and Jay found them. Finally I had seen enough.

"Let's go," I said.

We passed out through the bar to the dark plaza, where Otto sat rasping with the gypsies. "Otto," I called. "Do you want to come with us?" But Otto kept rasping so we crossed the plaza to the far end, where the walking street was crowded with bums. As we curved into the Old Town on the slope, I slowed.

"You want to see the cats?"

"No, they depress me."

We kept walking. "So what is it you want to talk about?"

"I don't know," he said. "Sometimes I just don't know."

"That tells me a lot." Overhead the sky glittered, and Per was giving me a headache. When I had first met him, his silence had fooled me, and I had thought he was a contented person. But he wasn't.

It is not circumstances outside that matter, it is the things inside, all the dark fuzzy inside things that no one can ever really see.

"It's getting chilly," Per said.

"Yes," I muttered.

"There's an extra room next to me if you want. Room for both you and Otto."

I turned to Per. In the moonlight a single tear shimmered on his cheek. Some things I would never understand. "Really?" I said.

"Really."

We kept descending til we reached the beachfront. The moon lit up the ocean crests and turned the sand to wedding gray. We sat on wooden lounge chairs and stared out to sea.

"What are you thinking about?" he asked.

"Nothing."

The moon rocked the waves and seagulls screeched around a jetty. I cupped my hands to my mouth and blew. It was getting cold.

"I think I'd like another drink," I said. I got up and stuffed my hands into my pockets.

"I'll stay here," he said. I started walking away. "Hey," he called. "When you going to move in?"

"Soon," I shouted back. "Maybe tomorrow."

For a week we writhed in our sleeping bags. The roar came back in Otto's voice and all the calm was gone. Then I moved in next to Per. Otto stayed on the bluff.

I had a sparse room with a small kitchen and bath, rent free. I was lucky. Money was drying up, and I didn't have much time left—maybe a month. I gave smaller tips at Charley's and his good humor faded. After a while I could afford only supermarket beer, and when I saw Charley on the plaza he waved me off. In the evenings, I stayed in my room.

The sounds held many mysteries. The opening and shutting of doors, hurried gasps of breath, mumbled dialogues barely rising above a whisper. Per always seemed to have visitors, but his bleak mood never improved. I would sit and drink beer until everything became blurry. Then I would fall asleep.

Sometimes Per would come over and we would have fumbled conversations. I was obliged, he was my landlord.

I did not like him very much because he reminded me of myself, all pent-up and depressed like a caged animal.

Money was really running low now and I took to panhandling a little. Not much. The gypsy children had a flower racket going. They sold stolen roses to the tourists on the plaza. I got a few kids together and ran the walking street cafes. They needed me to reach the roses off the bushes.

I tried to organize them. I had four kids, Paco and Julio and Maria and Bianca, all dark-skinned with pastel clothing, real gypsies. They each had a section of the walking street. I stationed myself in an alley near the middle, clutching a basket of roses.

I sent them out with no more than four roses each. Sometimes I sent them in pairs, always the girls together or the boys together, never mixed.

I gave them half of what they sold, and kept half for myself.

Some days they couldn't sell anything. I invested in some onions to make them cry, and that worked. But by Christmas few tourists remained.

I bought some candy canes cheap, and the kids sold them for a lot of money. A group of American sailors stopped here for two weeks. It became a science. The worse the kids looked, the better they sold.

After a while I took to feeding them lunch, a canned food or some leftovers I had swiped off a cafe table. Then I kept all the money and they didn't mind.

I got sick of it, though, and tried to sell some hash. But the gypsies wouldn't let me. "Too dangerous," they said.

"Be serious."

"All right. We've got to feed ourselves, too, you know. Face it, you're on vacation. We live here."

"Okay," I said. I stuck to roses and candy canes.

I made enough to drink a little more, that was it. The older gypsies stayed nice to me, though. I stopped selling at sunset, and sat on the plaza with them. We played checkers, huddled around a bunsen stove, passed bottles and pipes.

We didn't talk very much, but that was okay. I was leaving soon and had nothing to say. Otto amused them when it came to that, kept roaring except when the police passed. He seemed to know they would treat him badly.

And every night I would return to the room and fall into bed. Otto stayed on the plaza now, slept with the gypsies.

I could never fall asleep right away, so I could hear Per's mysteries through the wall. All the muffled sounds felt like listening to a theatre show from backstage.

three

I was listening to these sounds. The sliding of sandalled feet on the hallway. The knock of thick knuckles on Per's door. Per's low greeting. The other's greeting with a British accent. The opening and shutting of the door.

Two men almost whispering, talking so low.

The shuffle of clothes. The click of a night lamp. More whispers, whispers all the time. Threatening to rise to full voices, but not.

A giggle. A sigh. The click of a night lamp.

The clack of wooden-soled shoes on the hallway. The knock of knuckles on Per's door.

The click of a night lamp.

The silence of people waiting.

A low call from the hallway, Spanish accent.

The answer, British accent.

Giggles. The opening of Per's door. Laughter. The shutting of Per's door.

How many times must I recall this?

All right. Three men talking low now. A Spaniard, a Brit and Per.

The clink of glasses being taken out and handed around. The sound of liquid being poured.

A triple clink—a toast.

I tried to fall asleep, but I couldn't. Low talking kept

going.

I must have fallen asleep. It was dark all over, when I heard it. A cry so high and piercing it could have been a whistle, someone whooping air in pain.

People moving heavily in Per's room. Things bumping the wall, falling to the floor. A window opening. A Spaniard cursing.

Then the sound of feet running on the street below, the sandals and the wooden shoes. I got up and put my ear to Per's wall. Not a sound.

"Per," I called. "Per." But not a sound.

I opened my door and went out into the hallway and looked around, I don't know why. I walked down to Per's room and looked at the door. From the inside light I could see through the crack that it wasn't bolted. I called Per again, but no response.

I put my head to the door and listened for Per. But not a sound. It was all too still, and the cry. I had to look.

I opened the door. I don't know.

Per lying naked on the floor, all tied up in sheets or something. I don't know. Red all over his body like it had been fingerpainted on. His eyes all white and dead, sofa turned over, wine bottle empty at his neck.

His throat cut, I don't know.

four

We got our things together. It didn't take any time. The police helped, booked our train, stopped asking so many questions. Said I had been a big help. I don't know.

I stayed with Otto and the gypsies the last nights. We sat on the plaza, trying to smile at each other. Otto went dumb, didn't say anything. I was on tranquilizers, prescribed.

The gypsies didn't say much either, never did.

The morning of our train a police car drove onto the plaza. Otto and I got our stuff, and they settled us into the back seat.

We drove slowly out of the plaza, past Charley's Bar and the signs saying "Space for Rent," I don't know, past the gypsy kids carrying roses, past the last of the American sailors, and finally bumping down a couple steps to the road. To Malaga.

At the train station, dense with pigeons and people, they ushered us through to our train. There were some reporters, and they kept shouting questions at me and I said, I don't know, I don't know.

We got into our compartment, Otto and I, and shut the door up tight, drew the shades, and looked out the window at the reporters and police.

I looked at Otto and Otto looked at me. And he frowned. But didn't say anything.

The train started moving and the policemen waved and some of the journalists stared. All their faces started going by, and then the faces of people I'd never seen, and then the walls of the train tracks and finally the town itself. Malaga started going by and I looked at Otto and Otto looked at me. And in the slow rolling of the train he smiled.

PART III

one

This is it and we are back in it.

The Big Man sits at his table in Woodstock, surrounded by dogs. We walk in. He looks up, gives a happy cry.

"Good to see you," he says, on his feet now, holding us in his arms.

"I read about you in the papers," he says.

"It was very bad," I say.

"I can imagine."

We sit down with him and he continues his business. One kilo for you, half a kilo for you, two kilos for you, on and on after the long train ride. We are still rolling.

It is dead winter with homemade stoves and stolen wood.

"I've been keeping your house up for you," the Big Man says out of the side of his mouth. "Kept the snow out."

"Maybe we'll go there now," I say. "I'm very tired. Otto?"

But Otto is asleep on the table, will not budge.

I rise and nod, rise and nod.

Outside the sun melts the snow on Pusher Street, turns the cobblestone to quicksilver. "Hash!" someone shouts at me. "Great hash! I've just been to Morocco."

"Nepal! Excellent Nepal!" another shrieks.

I hurry past them and the crowd at the Grocer's, peek out of the corner of my eye at Moonfisher silent in the middle of the day, and vanish into the Magic Forest.

It is the same, all quiet and stiff and distant to the sky, looking for warmth. I pass no one except my shadow against the snow. Good to be back, I am telling myself.

And what are you telling yourself, Luna Daisyland?

I run, run, run to my home, go so fast that I lift off the ground, soar to the stars, nearly touch the moon. Then bellyflop down.

I am at the door now, pull myself in, lock the memories out behind me.

Just a home. The tapestry, the chest, the mattress— nothing more. The walls still upright, most cracks sealed with lime now. Thank you, Big Man.

The mattress again. I lie on it. It used to be such a small mattress. Now it is so big. I roll around it, fight for a moment. Then it comes and I can do nothing. I begin to cry and

The night. Cold and dark, teeth chattering. Rolling in and out of sleep, rolling around.

With the first sun, a late sun in the winter, a knock at the door.

"What?" I call, all tangled in the tapestry.

"It's me," a woman calls. "The Big Man told me you were back."

"Who?"

"Riina," she says. "Can I come in?"

I think about it for a minute.

"No," I finally say, return to rolling around the mattress, fighting everything.

Days later, I don't know. I finally leave the mattress and step outside, watch my breath gather and dissolve in the winter air, watch the trees and their shadows grow. Just watch.

I force myself to walk. First one foot, then the other, looking down at them making tracks in the snow. They go to Otto's, to the hammock in front of the Grocer's.

Otto is there, all right, growling, thundering. I go over and he looks at me.

"Whore Pity Beast Memories People Die," he says.

I shake him off. I love him but he can't always be right. I go to Woodstock.

"Ready to work?" the Big Man says.

"Okay." I get my brick of hash and go sit in the Common Kitchen, pick at the candlewax and say, "Good stuff. Really good stuff."

Otto joins me when it gets dark. It is as if we never left. Is that good or bad? The Big Man comes, too.

"Why'd you turn Riina away?" he asks. "You don't like her?"

"Too much," Otto roars, sends memories pinwheeling. "Really too much Spiral Churches."

"Exactly," I say.

"Half of life is sharing," says the Big Man. "That's why Luna Daisyland made you so happy. Why not share with Riina now?"

I shrug, sip a bottle of beer. Everyone is turning therapist on me.

Other people turn up, everyone: people from the search, Baker Whores. All forgiving. All forgetting. All dressed like gypsies, talking art or politics or sugar beets. But they buy me beer, and that's all I want.

"What do you think?" German Thomas asks me.

"About what?"

"They're talking again about closing Christiania."

I laugh. They always talk that. I take another sip and ignore him. Someone starts up a chillum, it comes to me and I take a long one. It goes right to my head, thank god, eases all the weight pressing down.

The Big Man studies me. I can feel it. I turn to look at him.

"I missed you," he says.

I think of what somebody once said. "I missed myself," I say.

Waking up with Riina in bed. Oh no. I roll over, roll back. She is still there. I clamp my eyes shut, feel her weight shift.

Finally she is up off my mattress. I don't remember anything. She's got tie-died long underwear on. Then she wraps a purple skirt around her, pulls on purple leggings,

75

lashes a purple scarf to her neck, adjusts her homemade earrings and says,

"Do you have a mirror?"

"No." I roll away.

I see the vanity of the world.

"You've got to break out of it," the Big Man is saying.

"Break out of what?"

"I don't know. I would say it was time for a trip, but you just came back."

"No more trips," I say.

"Maybe in the summer we'll go to Dragor."

"No."

The Big Man rises, smiles in a sad way. "You'll be all right," he says. "Some day."

I wake to a searing at my crotch. It burns from the inside out.

First I try to pack it with ice, but that doesn't help.

Then I try to wear clean underwear every day, but still it burns. Finally I go to the Health House. They refer me to a nearby VD clinic.

Riina, I am thinking.

At the clinic there are a lot of different looking people. Middle-aged women in clothes three shades of white. Young men sucking licorice sticks. Greenlanders in leather jackets. I take a number from the automatic dispenser, wait an hour. Then my number is announced over a loudspeaker and I go in.

A white room with a white sheet on a brown vinyl table.

"Drop your pants," a man in a white jacket says.

He examines me, prods, pulls, cajoles. Then he gives me a cup.

"Go urinate in it," he says. "Then call us in a couple days."

I call in a couple days. I have the clap; it is not funny. I want to tell Riina, I don't know why. I tell the Big Man.

"No problem," he says. "You'll get over it."

"It's Riina's fault."

"So?"

I go sit in my home and try to make the medicine work. But after two weeks it still burns. I return to the clinic. They do more tests. I call in a few days.

"You are cured," they say. "Forget about it."

But my crotch burns on.

The burning is like a ringing in my ears. After a while, I have felt it so long, I no longer feel it. But it is there, and when I think of it, I feel it.

It doesn't matter. I don't use it anyway.

two

They are surrounding us with cinderblocks.

From the inside out, I heard the roar of trucks. I got out of bed and looked around, saw nothing but the black forest on the brown melting snow.

I went out to the main entrance near the church. People everywhere. The Big Man. Otto. The Baker Whores. The Uro. Everyone. Danes in yellow helmets stood directing traffic and cranes. Cinderblock on top of cinderblock around Christiania.

Riina sidled up to me.

"Really too much," she said. "It's really too much."

German Thomas climbed atop a beer crate.

"Friends," he shouted. "It's happening. They're closing us down."

People laughed. "Get down," they said. "Shut up."

But I wasn't sure. I went to ask the Big Man. "What do you think?" I said.

"Don't know," he said. And walked away.

Me too. Just slipped back into the Magic Forest, and listened to the noise. Cinderblocks being shifted and prodded make a sound almost like wine glasses clinking. But soon it stopped, me lying here. Waiting.

A long time, I think. They'll have to come get me.

The Big Man enters.

"It smells dead in here," he says.

"Like outside."

"No." He sits down on the memory chest, smiles. "Not like outside."

"Is the cinderblock gone?"

"No." He sniffs the air again, winces. "We're surrounded. But nothing's happening." He smiles again. "Business as usual." He gets to his feet. "Come on, get up," he says.

I try to move my legs. Everything is numb, I've been lying here so long. "I can't," I say. "Help me."

The Big Man's little hand pulls me up, leans me over his back. The house compacts.

"What was that?" I ask.

"You threw up." He drags me outside. "Breathe deeply," he says.

"Shouldn't have stayed in bed so long." And then I am happy. Where is the burning, I am thinking. But then I think and there it is.

"We'll have a beer," the Big Man says. "That will help."

"Yes."

We walk for some time before I hear the shouting and singing. "Has there been a lot of it?" I nod at the sound.

"Enough," the Big Man says.

We get to Pusher Street and everyone is throwing tomatoes at each other. From the windows in the Common Kitchen I can see the cinderblock all around. The Big Man brings two Carlsbergs.

He sees me looking. "There's no barbed wire," he says. "No guards. No checkpoint. Just a lot of cinderblocks. No one's saying anything."

"Christ," I say, watching the table melt. Soon there is blood and I am face down in it.

The Big Man is pulling me back up, blood on my shirt and on my hands. "Nosebleed," he says. "You're as pale as the moon."

"Don't—" I try to hide, spin a little, and then everything is all over me and dark like rotten applesauce.

Cinderblock dreams.

I wake up in a white hospital bed in a white hospital room. Look around, but no policemen. Just the Big Man.

"Hello," he says.

"Hello," I say. "How am I?" I look at the ceiling, all pockmarked like last time, and at the endless row of windows, each with its own bed. I feel like nothing. I feel numb all over. The Big Man does not answer my question, just looks at the floor.

"How long I been asleep?"

"Not long. A half day."

"What do the doctors say?"

"Not much." The Big Man shrugs. "I can take you home when you're ready."

"What's the matter with me?"

"Don't know." The Big Man rises. "Let's get out of

here."

I crawl off the bed and find the floor. The Big Man hands me a bottle. "Painkillers," he says. "Compliments of the hospital."

We go to his whale. Otto is there, dressed in a new black overcoat, still dirty and rumpled, and a black ski hat. I lie down on the floor. The Big Man hands me a drink. Otto sniffs the air.

"Nice bracelet," the Big Man says.

I rip it off, my name and everything. I feel so tired.

"Why is Otto in black?" I ask the Big Man.

"He got tired of gray."

Otto grunts, forms words with his mouth but nothing comes. Then, "Clay Valley Shepherd No Want," he says.

I turn to the Big Man. The room spins but I stop it. The drink feels strange. Everything tastes like silver in my mouth. What Otto said.

"Am I dying?" I ask the Big Man.

"I don't know," he says. And turns away.

During the night my nose bleeds. The Big Man is there to stop it. All the lights are on but still the house feels very dark.

"I can take you back to the hospital," the Big Man says. "If you want."

"No." Otto lies next to me, snoring. "But we'll go to Christiania," I say. "Tomorrow."

"Tomorrow," the Big Man says. And he turns the lights out.

In the morning I feel better. Things are coming back to me. My tongue has its own taste, and my fingers no longer tingle. I stand up and my head clears and the Big Man laughs.

"Chillum?" he says.

"Why not."

Everything is fine and spring is strong. The sun lights up the Alfa Romeo and we are warm inside. Even Otto smiles. Then the Big Man turns to us and says, "We could go to Dragor," and everything goes bad inside.

"No," I say. "Just take us back."

He takes us back. It's all surrounded by cinderblock, five meters high. But inside it is still the same. Spring warms everything, the bonfires gone and the grass rising. We go to Moonfisher to celebrate.

I take a pill with the beer.

"Keep taking them," the Big Man says. "It can't hurt."

Soon I am feeling fine. "Should I sell today?"

"If you want. Make some money—it'll relax you."

I make money. It is spring and everyone wants to get high with it. German Thomas and Riina organize an "experience." They gather volunteers and begin painting the cinderblock lavender and turquoise.

At night we go to The Rag to hear an oboe concerto. Everything seems so real to me, as if I touch it just by seeing it. But I don't stay late, I feel too weak.

The Big Man offers to go home with me, or take me home with him. But I go home alone. A nice spring night, not too warm, the air thick around you like you can feel it, too, feel everything.

I get to my home and open the door. It is not too bad. Then lying on the mattress, so big after all. Then

In the morning it is very bad. Not the pain, but the thoughts. I get out of bed in a hurry and rush out to meet the sky.

A nice day, the sky blue like paint. In the far corner hangs the day moon. I look at it, try to face it, but it does not work. I count the stones walking to Pusher Street.

I am so early there is no one to sell to. Around eleven it picks up and I make money. But then it is noon and the siren goes and the dogs howl. I haven't been here for noon in such a long time, since that last time. Can't get up that early, thank god. But now I'm here with everyone else. Howling at the noon moon.

The Big Man shows up for office hours, claps me on the back, looks me up and down like a statue. Otto, too, explores me.

"You look better," the Big Man says.

"Yes," I say.

"I'm glad." He strolls off with his hands in his pockets, followed by his dogs. Otto stays with me, explores himself. He fingers his new coat, strokes his beard, sighs loudly, picks his nose, and watches me. I sell well despite him, and buy him beers while we wait for the crowd to stop. Like always, so many people on such a nice day.

Late spring and most of summer go like this, smooth and fast. We are in control.

There is a solution to the night loneliness. I drink a lot. Everybody does, but I drink more, and on top of the morphine, it is really something. I almost never think past sunset.

The summer crowds are getting me down. But I like the money, gives me the feeling that I am counting toward something, that days are passing to a certain date, that there is a goal, I don't know what—it just gives that feeling.

The painting project also is taking a long annoying time. Now they're into jade and honey. Sometimes, to tease me, Riina will come spilling paint on my shoes. But I am too real. I never laugh.

Summer takes the longest time. The tourists and the groovies together make it go slowly. When I don't sell, Otto and I hide out in my home. I am feeling better. With the sun filtered on the wall like a rainbow, everything smiles.

Sometimes Riina or German Thomas stops by, and

things go bad. Riina wants to fuck me. German Thomas wants to politicize me. She says it is a time for sex—summer and the sun. He says it is a time for conflict—with autumn they will turn us all out of Christiania. I play passive and they go away. But they come again, come again, and are not scared by Otto's roars.

What can we do, waiting for summer to pass? We can't go outside, because that is where everyone is. Staying inside with our rainbow is all right, but a little warm. But here we are. For amusement we count my money. So much of it, it is really something.

We are still waiting. It makes me tired. I sleep for half-days, and still I wake up feeling sleepy.

"You are depressed," the Big Man says.

"It's the crowd," I say. If only they were cats.

"You could go away again."

"No." I sink into the mattress. "I will wait it out."

We count money. I have piles of bills rolled up in my tapestry.

"You should put it in your chest," the Big Man says.

"I can't," I say. "It won't open."

"Sure it will." He starts to lift the lid.

"Don't—" I fall on top of the chest, not wanting it all now, but getting it. "It's my memory chest," I say. They are coming up through my stomach now. I have to shift around, the way it's meant to be done.

"You—"

"Leave me alone," I tell him. Then everything is all inside and I can't

Clouds gather and rains come, but I can't get my body to do the things I want to do. Dizzy nearly all the time and the taste of silver comes back, coats my mouth and reaches down my throat. There is still morphine left but it is not working like it used to.

Now that all the people are gone, I must sleep. Really sleep.

three

I have never been this weak before. It is an experience. I begin to value when I can get up in the morning. Sometimes I can, and sometimes I can't.

Numb and tingling like my body has nothing left inside it anymore.

The Big Man comes as I am stuck in bed.

"You've got to get up," he says.

"Why?"

His hands wring around the room. "They're closing us down," he says.

I can't get up. But Otto is here and thinking quickly. He leaves and returns with a low wooden wagon, lifts me up but says nothing, wraps my tapestry and all its bills around me and we are ready. He rolls me out and the Big Man follows at my head.

It is a bumpy ride to Pusher Street but I do not mind.

I raise my head and see it all from my rolling coffin. People everywhere, stacked up the steps of the Common Kitchen and seeping out the doors of Woodstock. Black leather jackets and mauve shepherd coats all mixed up like a meeting at Circus Hall. No one selling. Everyone talking.

No Uro, either.

They all come up to the Big Man, ask him questions and tug his arm.

"It is very simple," he says, pointing out to the cinderblock. "No one can enter, but anyone can leave."

More talk. Looking up at all of them from my wagon, I can see their nostril hairs.

"Once you leave you cannot return," the Big Man adds.

Otto rolls me out to the wall and we take a look. Uro posted every fifty meters on top, and coils of barbed wire thick around them.

The Big Man is with us.

"What happens if we just stay in here?" I ask.

"Nothing," he says. He points at all the placards posted on the trees and the inside of the wall. "They'll let supplies in. But you can't ever leave and come back. It'll be like prison."

"But they won't bother us if we stay inside?"

"They're not supposed to."

Otto rolls me back to Pusher Street. The Big Man feeds me beer through a straw.

"How do you feel?" he asks.

"All right."

We keep vigil with everyone else on Pusher Street. Fires blaze. The sky overhead is as clear as water. It is very cold and nothing happens. It is not the season for tourists anyhow.

By the evening it's just a lot of cigarettes and magazines. No music hums from the rock bars. They are already closed down. Some of the people on Pusher Street lean on their packed bags, looking like they're waiting for a train. Already there is a small line funneling out the exit gate.

Otto wheels me home to sleep. The Big Man stays on Pusher Street, pondering.

"It has never been that great a thing," he says. "So not much can be lost."

The next morning, with all the leaves off the trees and the wind sweeping the cobblestone, already we have dwindled. By noon I have some strength and climb out of the wagon to sit at a table with the Big Man. Even the siren howl seems less crowded. Those who have left have taken their dogs.

"I think we should do something," German Thomas says.

"No," says the Big Man. "There is nothing we can do. They give us a choice, and we make it. It seems pretty fair." He grows philosophical, expands before us like some great solid balloon. "When I'm ready," he says, "I'll go, too."

Moonfisher closes. To celebrate they set the building on fire. We all go over there to keep warm. Flames lick at our faces and the Uro from the walls make no attempt to stop them. The owner hands out little candy canes and chocolate hearts.

"Merry Christmas," he says.

It's only November.

We sit outside the Common Kitchen. They are burning the bakery now and there is a roar of fire when the ovens explode. Ashes sift through the air like snowflakes. The Big Man reflects.

"They waited til the tourist season finished," he says, "and then, when no one cared, they closed us down. Very good."

"Like I said all along," German Thomas says.

"Yes," says the Big Man. "Like you said all along."

The windows of the bakery implode. I catch Otto's grin before he hides it.

I lie in bed. My wagon-hearse-coffin attends me outside my door, ready to roll me down to Pusher Street for another day of fire watching. Otto still sleeps on his hammock in front of the Grocer's. The Big Man stays up all night, all day. He says he can sleep when he leaves. He fuels himself with whiskey and cigarettes like I have never seen. I am glad he is still here.

Otto comes to get me in the morning, roaring at my door. Foreign languages again. Except every now and then "Seventh Day Noah" seeps through the Latin or Greek.

We roll down to Pusher Street. The Big Man is looking all shriveled up inside. "I can't stay and lose money like this," he says. "I have to go."

"To Amsterdam?" I keep my voice from breaking.

"Maybe not. Maybe I can sell in Vesterbro." He looks at the ground. I fall back in my wagon and look at the sky, white and thick like whipped cream.

"It may snow," I say.

"Maybe," the Big Man says. "I've got to get going." He reaches down and touches my shoulder. I hold his hand for a moment. It feels soft but steady, like a spring leaf.

"Good-bye," I say, letting go.

"Good-bye." He turns and leaves, a lot of the pushers following him out like an army of ants. I lie back again, looking at the sky and hearing Otto's raspy breathing. I shut my eyes for a moment, hoping. Then open them. Everything is still here. But not everyone.

Otto takes me and props me up against the steps of the Common Kitchen. The bills in the tapestry crackle when he moves me. The street's almost deserted now, the burnt buildings lying in their open graves. No pushers left, either. Now it is only the anarchists and Otto and me. We are the only ones not wearing purple.

They sit in a group around a fire, looking determined. German Thomas sometimes says something, and Riina giggles, and Dan and the others make Uro jokes. They act like they're doing somebody a favor by staying. They stay on principle. I stay on practice. I can't stand them.

After a while someone finds a guitar and they start singing peace songs. Stuff I haven't heard in years. I look out at the wall and notice film cameras peering in at us.

In the late afternoon the front gate opens and a truck drives in. An Uro drives the truck. At Pusher Street he stops. The owner of the Common Kitchen comes out, and, without looking at each other, they exchange money for food, food for money. The Uro gets back in his truck, locks the door, drives back out the gate. No one has said anything. There are not enough of us to cause a scene.

Otto and I buy some bread and sausage, and retreat to the Magic Forest. Here it feels like nothing is happening. We are missing no one because only the no one's live here. Otto spreads mustard on the bread and piles it thick with sausage. He opens a bottle of beer with his teeth and spreads everything before me. I love him all over again.

When he leaves to go to his hammock, the door opens wide and snow flutters in. Our first of the year.

I lie awake listening to the real night sounds. The creaking of the ice as it forms and breaks, forms and breaks, on Ostrich Lake. The death of a limb snapping off a tree. The breathing of fresh snow on the ground. No moon tonight, either. Everything just dark and rich.

It goes on like this for a while. We are almost happy. If only the purple people would leave. Then all my pain would be gone, and the only thing left would be the real pain inside of me—instead of all this people pain.

It hurts to watch these lavender impostors milking film footage from faraway cameramen, singing songs meant for crises. They trivialize the experience.

Today the Uro delivering food brought a letter. He got out of the truck and shouted my name. I waved a hand and he gave me an envelope.

I opened it and read. "Settled in Vesterbro. Nice place for you and Otto. Please Come." The Big Man. I said nothing and passed it to Otto. Who ate it, I don't know why.

There is a point between something and nothingness that feels like all your breath is gone, even though it keeps on coming.

Something new. Handbills posted, saying the Uro will do a sweep tomorrow to remove all the invalids and drunkards. Only the healthy are allowed to remain. For the good of everyone, it says.

I don't know whether Otto understands. I point and tell him. He grunts and nods like a prehistoric man. But goes to work. He brings the wagon-hearse into my home and sits and tinkers. First removes the wheels and stares a long time. Goes out and comes back again with a sled. Nails the wagon-hearse to the top of the sled and grunts speculatively.

We go out for a ride. With the snow thick on the ground, it is really something. We skid across Ostrich Lake to the sugar beet collective, all frozen and iced like tundra. Then down a slope into Milk Valley, across an open meadow and zooming now, Otto running beside me it seems, no longer tugging, til we crack on the cobblestone of Pusher Street. I am all out of breath.

I give Otto money and he goes into the Common Kitchen. Returns with a liter of whiskey, ten tins of mackarel and a loaf of rye bread.

He pulls me back to the Magic Forest and carries me to bed. Leaves immediately. Tomorrow will be a hard day. I want it, want sleep now, want to stay with Otto here forever.

The helicopters begin before we do, bobbing in the air like soap bubbles. I lie on my sleigh looking up at them. Otto hugs the side of the house. We wait until they head away, then slide down through some icy thorns and rumble along the canal.

The sky spreads bright blue with specks of gray over Christianshavn. We twist further into the forest, but beyond it there is only cinderblock at the outer rim.

Otto lopes along, tugging me. In the distance a loudspeaker goes, "Please assemble at the Common Kitchen. If you cannot walk, shout out and we will find you."

We labor on. An arrow of sweat creases Otto's back. I can see his back and ahead and the sky above me. But everything from the surface is so distorted. I am too close to it.

We keep to the back woods. There is so much noise but we see no one. The trick is avoiding the helicopters. If he stands a certain way in his black coat, Otto looks like a tree trunk. My tapestry is turned inside out to muted colors.

The sun crawls across the sky to the town. Sounds recede and Otto rests longer, more easily in one spot, it seems. We drink whiskey to keep warm. When the sun goes we open the mackarel and have dinner. Otto always spreading and cutting things, taking care of me. No longer roaring, not ever roaring, but humming thickly in his throat.

I have never been my own dog. Otto is my dog. Too obvious that dog spelled backwards is god and god spelled backwards is dog and Otto spelled backwards is Otto always.

At night I hear him breathe. He fills the air thick like smoke from a chimney. I am breathing with him, can't sleep, am too excited.

The sun comes up with Otto's hands at my cheeks, rubbing them. He grins and roars Latin at my eyes.

I am so cold I am warm.

We spend all day in my home, keeping warm. But then there is no more food and we have to go down to Pusher Street. I try to stand but I can't. Yet I am feeling so good, I don't understand. Otto lifts me to the sleigh and we slide down into the Common Kitchen.

The sky overhead is deep and dark. Even though it is snowing, I can see the moon. I feel so different about it now, as it comes closer. Not a symbol, but a person.

There are many things you can hide from yourself. But this slow winding down and happy clarity. I know it is something special, and not at all so terrible as it's supposed to be.

Pusher Street is quiet and coated with a new snow. The Common Kitchen gapes black and burnt, all gone. Only a few of the purple people are left, and they hold bags and boxes, are edging away.

"You're here?" German Thomas says.

"Of course." A little silence.

"You're going," I say hopefully.

"Yes." He looks down at the bright white snow, then around at all the darkness. "There's not enough people left," he says. "It's too boring."

They walk off and are soon gone.

It is night time with the moon through the clouds lighting up the snow. Everything burns bright and white. I prop myself up and look around, feel the place glowing in my mind.

And up at the shadow-ghost. It is bright and white and round and beautiful. It is Luna and she is the moon.

I look at Otto and he feels it, too. Just the three of us. He lifts me out of the sleigh and holds me to him. We look around together, all the bright light everywhere, like a happy desert. Just us.

His throat growls, and his voice turns soft and clear.

I hear him from a growing distance, through waves

on a beach or clouds in a sky. "Welcome to Christiania,"
he says.

I am somewhere fine.

Acknowledgments

I am grateful for the support of a Fulbright Scholarship during the drafting of this work.

Special thanks to Kathryn Rhett, for her unstinting encouragement, critical eye, and everything else under the sun and the moon.

Also, thanks to Eduardo and Karen and their three kids for returning to Christiania with us in 2009.

A brief excerpt of this work appeared in *Open City*. Thanks to Tom Beller and Joanna Yas.

And many thanks to Jon Roemer!

About the author

Fred Leebron has published several novels and numerous short stories, and has received both a Pushcart Prize and an O. Henry Award; he is also co-editor of *Postmodern American Fiction: A Norton Anthology* and co-author of *Creating Fiction: A Writer's Companion*. He directs writing programs in Charlotte, Roanoke, Europe, Latin America, and Gettysburg.